Yes I Can!

Have My Cake and Food Allergies Too

Written by
Julie Wethington

Illustrated by
Lang Wethington

DragonWing BOOKS

www.DragonWingBooks.com

Love you!
Julie Wethington

Best, Lang Wethington

Like many kids his age, Jack hears the word "NO" a lot.
And he listens… sometimes.

But there is one "NO" that Jack always listens to. It is his number one rule: **"No eating anything unless you ask Mommy or Daddy first."**

This is very important because Jack has food allergies. If he eats even a tiny bit of a food he is allergic to, he gets very sick. Or worse yet, he may even have to get a shot and go to the hospital. Yikes! Jack does NOT want that to happen.

At the grocery store, Jack's mommy and daddy read all the labels. If they see the words "MILK," "EGG," or "PEANUT," they know that the food is not safe for Jack. Jack can't wait to be old enough to read the labels all by himself.

The good news is that Jack also hears the word "YES" a lot. Jack has food allergies, but he also gets to eat lots of delicious foods and do lots of fun things. In fact, Jack has a very exciting weekend ahead of him.

On Friday, Jack and his friends get together for a playgroup. The mommies make snacks that all the children can enjoy. They have grapes, animal crackers, carrot sticks, and **– oh boy – homemade banana muffins!**

But just to be safe…

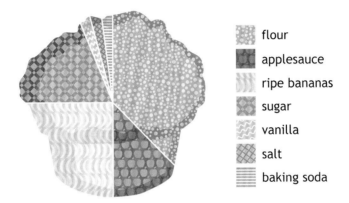

flour
applesauce
ripe bananas
sugar
vanilla
salt
baking soda

Jack asks his Mommy, "Can I have a muffin?"
"Yes, you can," she answers.

On Saturday morning, Jack and his parents go to their favorite museum. They spend hours exploring all the cool stuff, like fossils and dinosaur bones.

As they pass by the museum's restaurant, the yummy smells make Jack feel hungry. "Can we eat our picnic now?" he asks.

"Yes, we can," his parents answer.

Cafe

Jack's family often brings their food when they go out, because sometimes restaurants don't have food that is safe for Jack. Also, it's fun to have picnics!

Jack, Mommy, and Daddy enjoy the sunshine as they eat a tasty lunch of sandwiches, cherries, pretzels, applesauce, and homemade chocolate chip cookies…

made by Mommy, of course!

Later that afternoon, Jack and his daddy go to the playground. Jack races to join the fun. Suddenly, the jingling tune of the ice cream truck can be heard coming up the street. The other kids scream with joy and run toward the sound.

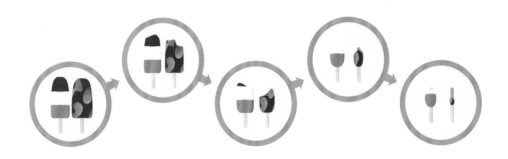

"Can I have ice cream too?" Jack asks.
Daddy sees that some of the popsicles are safe for Jack.
"Yes, you can," Daddy answers,
and they each pick out their favorite flavors.

On Sunday, there is a birthday party for Jack's mommy. All of Jack's grandparents, aunts, uncles, and cousins are there. Everyone brings a dish to share, and presents for Mommy!

When it's time to open presents, Jack's
mommy receives a beautiful bracelet.

"Look Mommy, it's just like mine!" Jack says proudly.
His bracelet is extra cool because it gives information
about his allergies, and it has a snake on it!

For dinner, there is so much food to choose from.
"Daddy, can you help me pick out foods that are
safe for me to eat?" asks Jack.

"Sure, buddy," Daddy answers. He fills Jack's plate with fruit salad,
baked beans, chips, and a juicy hamburger covered in ketchup. When
Jack is finished eating, he is completely stuffed!

But when cake time comes, Jack forgets all about feeling stuffed. Mommy blows out the candles on the big chocolate cake and winks at Jack, because Mommy and Jack share a secret!

He helped Mommy bake the cake following their special
family recipe, using only safe ingredients. So when Mommy
asks the biggest, most important question of all,

"Can you eat this cake, Jack?"

Jack laughs happily and cheers…

"Yes I can!"

For Jack

Text Copyright © 2012 by Julie Wethington
Illustrations Copyright © 2012 by Lang Wethington

All rights reserved. No part of this book may be reproduced, transmitted, or stored in any information retrieval system in any form or by any means, graphic, electronic, or mechanical, including photocopying, taping, and recording, without prior written permission from the publisher.

First Edition 2012
Library of Congress Control Number 2012930738
Wethington, Julie & Lang
Yes I Can! Have My Cake And Food Allergies Too / Julie & Lang Wethington – 1st ed.

Summary: A boy with food allergies learns ways to stay safe. Can he enjoy a weekend of tasty food and fun activities? Yes, he can!

ISBN 0-9761444-1-7
(1. Individuality – Fiction. 2. Food allergies – Fiction. 3. Family – Fiction. 4. Confidence – Fiction.)

The illustrations were produced using ink and watercolor and arranged using digital media.
The typeset is Carnegie

Published by DragonWing Books

Columbia, Maryland 21045
www.DragonWingBooks.com

Printed in China

10 9 8 7 6 5 4 3 2 1